For Luca and Ella with love
S. M.

Coventry City Council	
CCS	
3 8002 02204 874 0	
Askews & Holts	Jan-2015
	£10.99

First published in 2015
by Nosy Crow Ltd
The Crow's Nest, 10a Lant Street
London SE1 1QR
www.nosycrow.com

ISBN 978 0 85763 249 4 (HB)
ISBN 978 0 85763 250 0 (PB)

A CIP catalogue record for this book is available from the British Library.

Printed in China
Papers used by Nosy Crow are made from wood grown in sustainable forests.

10 9 8 7 6 5 4 3 2 1 (HB)
10 9 8 7 6 5 4 3 2 1 (PB)

Love Always Everywhere

Sarah Massini

nosy crow

Love me

Love you

Love one

Love two

Love quiet

Love loud

Love shy

Love proud

Love lose

Love miss

Love smile

Love kiss

Love tickle

Love snug

Love care

Love share

Love always . . .

. . . every

where.